T0193576

The Adventures
of
SADIE

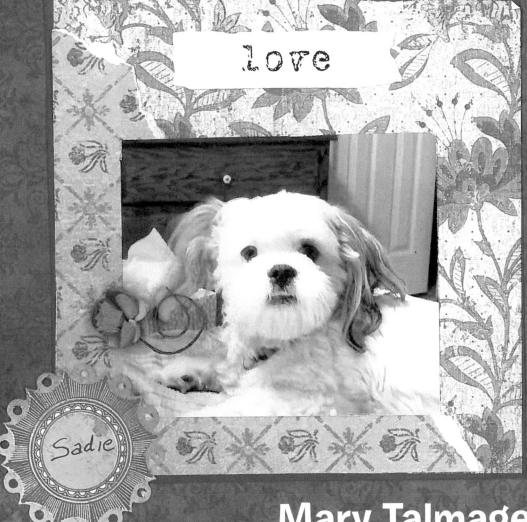

Love

Sadie

Mary Talmage

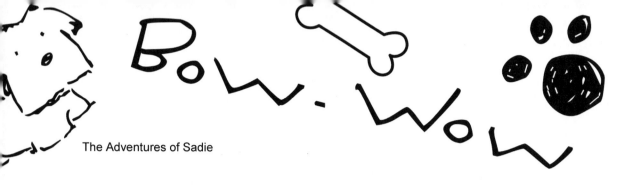

BOW-WOW

The Adventures of Sadie

iUniverse books may be ordered through booksellers or by contacting:

iUniverse
1663 Liberty Drive
Bloomington, IN 47403
www.iuniverse.com
844-349-9409

ISBN: 978-1-6632-0826-2 (sc)
ISBN: 978-1-6632-0827-9 (e)

Library of Congress Control Number: 2020916775

Print information available on the last page.

iUniverse rev. date: 09/15/2020

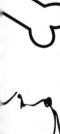

Sadie at the beach.

Bow-Wow

Tummy

Tummy rub?

Adventures
of
Sadie

Tummy rub?

The journey

Sadie was so excited as Mom put on her leash. She had watched Mom and Dad pack the car for a trip. She knew they were going somewhere. Mom put the picnic basket in the car and excitement was growing. Then they put her in the car. She could see everything and with the window down could feel the wind on her face. Everybody was ready so, they all headed out.

They started driving and there were all kinds of smells and noises. The car was moving smoothly and gently and soon Sadie fell asleep. A car door popped open and Sadie woke up. She realized they were at Grandpa's house at the beach!

Tummy rub?

Bow. Wow

Tummy rub?

Granpa's house

It was Grandpa's house, where the entire backyard belonged to Sadie for her to run and play in. In the backyard Sadie could go anywhere she wanted. She could smell anything she wanted, and she could see all of her friends.

Tummy rub?

Sam

Sadie ran to the water and got her paws wet, then ran back up to a rusty old post to see her friend Sam the seagull. Sadie said "Hello Sam how are you doing" Sam replied "Great Sadie, it's good to see you. Would you like some fish to eat?" Sadie said "Yes and thank you for sharing." "Do you know if Cecil is in his usual spot today?" asked Sadie. Sam answered "Yes, Cecil is in his favorite spot by the dock." "You should go and see him."

Tummy rub?

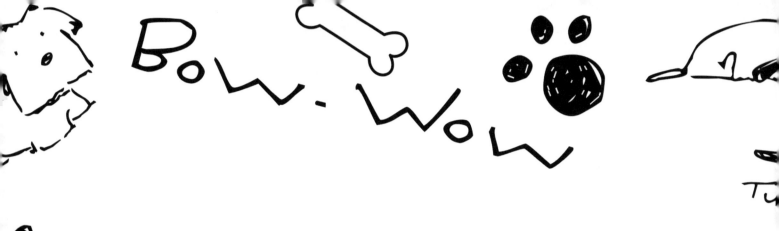

Cecil Sealion

Sadie ran down to the very very end of the dock, where Cecil was swimming. Cecil said "Hi Sadie." "How are you doing?" Sadie said "Good!" "What has brightened your day today? Cecil rolled over in the water and answered Sadie "seeing you made me shine today." "Plus, you surprised me with your visit." "I can always count on you to cheer me up." "Thanks for making my day a great one." Sadie said, "You cheer me up too!" "I better go check on Curtis and see you again soon."

Tummy rub?

Curtis Crab

Sadie decided to walk under the pier and, suddenly saw, her friend Curtis the Crab. Sadie wished him well and asked him "Could you help me with a problem?" Curtis said "of course Sadie, what is bothering you?" Sadie said "I saw the flowers Mom brought Grandpa." "What can I give Grandpa?" "hmm" pondered Curtis. "Just by being here is a gift." "Just show him your love for him." Sadie thought for a minute and said "Thank you so much Curtis you always know how to help."

Tummy rub?

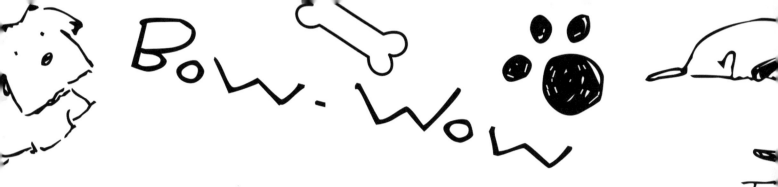

Goldie the Golden Retriever
(Sadie by the water)

Sadie wandered over to the other side of the backyard to see Goldie, the Golden Retriever. After the grass ran out there was nothing but warm soft sand on her paws. Goldie was tucked away in his own little house. It was painted blue with white trim. Sadie ran up to Goldie and they touched noses. Next, they ran down the beach and splashed in the ocean. Sadie said to Goldie, "Do you think we would ever get tired of the ocean?" Goldie paused and said "I don't think so." "The ocean was here before Grandpa. And Grandpa is really old." "Besides the ocean is such a big part of everything in our lives." "We are so blessed to have it."

Tummy rub?

Grandpa

She heard a whistle and her name being called. There was Grandpa, Sadie ran up to him and wagged her tail. Sadie knew this was a good way to show Grandpa how much she loved him. He looked down and petted Sadie and slipped her a cookie! Grandpa then whispered to Sadie "you make my heart shine." Two legs or more, good friends make you shine, and feel the love we all share.

Tummy rub?

Bow-Wow

Sadie was so tired from all of the adventures, she slept the whole way home. She dreamed of sharing fish with Sam and renewing her friendship with Cecil. She also dreamed about the advice from Curtis, and playing with Goldie. And the best part was sharing her love with Grandpa.

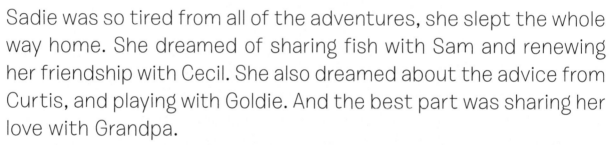

Tummy rub?